I0649089

Over The Horizon

A poetic love story based on my life

By

Roland Esco

Copyright © 2007 by Roland Esco

All rights reserved. No part of this work may be reproduced or used in any form by any means – graphic, electronic, or mechanical, including photocopying, recording, taping or any information storage and retrieval system – without written permission of the author.

Front Cover Photo: by Roland Esco

Back Cover Photo: by Judy V.

Published by: ProComOne.com

ISBN – 978-0-6151-6146-4

Special Mentions

Erin Nichole Kartis, LPN or RN
May she find happiness and true love one day in the horizons of time

Silas and his beloved wife Florence
For the inspiration of love and appreciation of the Torah

Gerrit
For being the brother I never had

Judy
For being the sister I never had

Isabel and Mariano
For their help and advice

Hernando
For his patience and doing me favors

Jasper
My cat, for being my furry friend as I wrote this

I would enjoy sharing with my readers their thoughts about
the novel or of your own stories of love, joy and heartbreak.
roland@procomone.com
http://www.myspace.com/RolandEsco

About the author

This is based on a true story and parallels many events in my life. A few things have been changed for the purpose of story line continuity, but the message and subject matter has not been altered. The old man in my story is real and he is my good friend and my inspiration for much of this. She is also very real and somewhere out there maybe standing beside you or walking past you all the while having never read a word of her letter or any of this.

The first book I was going to write was going to be a technical book I had been doing research on for a long time which was to be a law enforcement guide on the convergence of the Internet and encryption technology and their potential for misuse. I have always had an interest in researching and writing about bizarre and esoteric topics from various themes.

There are no names of people and few mentions of place or time, because love in the horizons of time is timeless and this can be anyone of us, one day you could be her or me. A love story is only between two people and that's all that should matter.

A woman of valor who can find? For her price is far above rubies.

The heart of her husband doth safely trust in her, and he hath no lack of gain.

Torah
Proverbs 31:10-11

Table of Contents

Bliss

In the flickering light of the candle and the night's steady warm and humid southern tropical ocean breeze, I helped the old man from his chair, as he struggled to stand with wobbly legs. Gently I coaxed him to place his arm over my shoulder, and as he arose from the chair his robe brushed against my chest releasing the scent of the woman that he loved. It was the rosy scent of the perfume his wife wore and this brought back memories for me, as I paused for a moment and remembered her as I stood in a small oval mirror on the wall beside the kitchen table.

The old man glanced up at me and realized what I was doing, and he then told me she was a beautiful woman with the blinding passion of the sun. I remembered how sweet she was to me, always baking and offering me something to eat. Often she would complement me on what a good and kindhearted person I am, and how happy I would make someone one day.

In the hallway the shadows shifted in waves of light from the candle down at end of the hall in the bedroom. With an unsteady gate, we both slowly staggered down the hall as if we were on a ship at sea. On the wall there were some of the family pictures, and as we walked by each of them he would pause for a minute to catch his breath and then look over at them in remembrance, as he could see his reflection in the glass of the picture frames.

Often he reminds me of being the adventuresome type, and of a time when he was young and daring enough to experience life overseas in distant lands. He was very lucky to have survived the hostile terrain and met his wife in such a desolate place. It all came as a surprise to him, one day when he least expected it.

That night it was what he wanted, to have only candlelight's in remembrance of his beloved wife for the Sabbath. Once long ago it was the light of a candle that brought them together, so it was fitting tribute. Slowly and with great care I helped him remove her robe, but before I even got the first arm out he asked me to neatly place it on her side of the bed. There was an uneasiness that I could feel in his breathing, as it was gradually becoming more pronounced as I slipped one arm out followed by the other. When I finally slipped it off, I heard a faint sigh as if he stood naked before the world in his pajamas, but what was nude to the world for all to see was his aching heart for his beloved wife.

With care I draped her robe over my shoulder and helped him to sit on the bed, then I lifted his feet over on to the bed as he laid back on the pillows. The old man heard the faint sound of a whistle from a train passing by on the other side of the bay, as it could be heard in the distance getting farther away. Even if it was a quiet night, he has not been able to sleep much since his wife's passing and all train whistles grow fainter with each passing day without her.

On the other side of the bed I neatly laid out her robe as he asked of me. His head touched the pillow beside her robe and he closed his eyes. Then, as if from his dreams, he kindly reminded me to bring him some tea.

There I was, young and full of vitality with a vast zest for life and all the good and bad it had to offer. Once again I would find myself running to her in my dreams, as I left the room with my eyes weighing heavily, since I had also not been sleeping very well at that time. It was a perfect convergence of stormy circumstances, as I was completing my final exams, when the woman I loved and whom I hoped to be my future fiancé decided to bring our relationship to an end. This made the moment bittersweet, as I was just about to begin my medical career.

Having made it just the way his wife did, or so I think, I brought him some tea. I hoped it was going to be just right, because earlier that evening I found it somewhat of a challenge preparing tea in the candlelight of the kitchen. She would prepare it with a drop of honey, just the way he liked it and I was hoping I got it right. Then as if I was looking at myself, when I walked into the bedroom he was sound asleep having the robe clutched and pressed against his cheek.

I could really sympathize with what he was doing, because since my fiancé left I also found myself laying in bed wide awake until dawn and then dozing off with her pillow. Obvious as it was to me, I knew the kind of memories that he was reminiscing of in his mind, for they were my own. That first kiss, that first smile, that first laugh, and that first crying tear they shared. There I stood in the doorway, looking at him as if I was reading his deepest thoughts, as if they were my own from a distant horizon of time, for they were. The thought of awakening him and taking him from such bliss is something that could not be beared not even in dreams. Since it was still early in the evening, I decided to stay a while, so if by chance he awoke I could bring him his tea.

As I made my way back to the kitchen down the hall, I really started to think about all the thoughts we shared between his readings of the Torah and sharing his life story in the warm glow of the candlelight. Since I am not Jewish and I do not understand the Hebrew religion very well he would read a few passages then explain their meaning to me.

Despite having been raised a Catholic I am not very religious, but I do appreciate the wisdom of the Bible from what I can remember from those Sunday school days as a child in the distant past. It was my first time I had ever been exposed to Hebrew scripture in my life, but as he read the passages and explored their elucidations with me I soon began to see their beautiful wisdom in life.

Sitting in the kitchen chair in front of those holy scriptures that are thousands of years old, I could not help but to stare at them in awe at how enlightening and inspiring they were to me. I began to introspect my own life and my relations with her and I understood what the old man was telling me, about what she most feared in life.

There was no misunderstanding, she was very explicit in her request that I leave her alone, because I did try to contact her several times, but each time her response was to leave her alone. I felt very strongly that I should honor her wishes and it had been a few weeks since the last time I tried to contact her as I was well on my way to never doing so again, but there was just something that came over me as I stared into the glimmering embers of the candlelight just beside those scriptures.

Trying to combat the urge of my meandering mind was a futile losing battle that I could not win, and I began to think there may have been something left unsaid and then suddenly I thought of the dread I might have years from now, if I were to look back and wonder if I really did what I could, and possibly have changed what my life would have been. The thought of living with such regret and always wondering about what could have been, "If only I had done something different?" and thus it was an unbearable sentence for which I could not endure the pain.

Infinite thoughts were surging through my head and before I realized it, I was hovering over a piece of paper on the table with a pen nervously in my hand and with the tip just itching the paper for the first thought. The words then started to flow like the natural wondrous waterfalls of the earth.

The Letter

You may think that I'm writing you this as an attempt to reconcile, but that is not the case. I am writing you this because I want you to be able to allow yourself to be loved the next time you find someone. After you left I have thought about things more then I ever have in my life. I don't know why you suddenly became so mean towards me and left. I have been spending a lot of time sharing thoughts with an old Jewish man since his wife passed away. We spend Fridays together as he reads passages from the Torah and then he explains their meaning to me.

The old man told me what you are most afraid of and he also told me about the importance of having trust and patience as a virtue. Even though I am not religious at all, because I went to Catholic schools and later to Jewish schools all my life, there is something ingrained in me that I can only give myself to a woman if she means a great deal to me. It is a paradox that in some ways I am experienced and in others I am naive about. I think because of being brought up this way even though I am 35 I have only had 3 girlfriends before you, from when I was 17 to 21, then from the age of 22 to 29, then from age 30 to 32, and for over 3 years now since I decided to leave the corporate world for a new start at a medical career, I have been alone. I did not realize what being alone for so long would do to me, so even though I am able to please you at times I think this has made me difficult to please, because I felt you no longer trusted me and I could not just rush my emotions, and it had been so long since I felt the feeling of the touch of a woman, and what I needed was to take things slow with patience and understanding from you.

There was one night when I asked you, "Did we just?" This is because of my inexperience and it had been so long since I had been with a woman that I didn't think I would know the difference or be able to feel the difference. It was simply a naive silly question and I did not imply that I wanted to do anything else other than my desire to do anything to please you. My only preference was to please you the way you wanted to be pleased. I am sorry that I was not experienced enough for you or anything else that I may have said all in an effort to please you. I hope that maybe you will grow from this and be patient and understanding with someone else one day in order for them to make you happy.

Anything that you may have read or seen while sitting at my desk is from a world of fiction and does not have any bearing on reality and does not change the way I feel about you, because I love you and I would never have left you for anyone else, nor would I have ever been unfaithful to you.

I know you are a good person with a good heart and I know that's the real you and not the one that's mean and unkind or selfish. He told me you become that way to protect yourself, but you did not need to be this way with me because I would never do anything to hurt you because the hurt that you feel coming from me is a misperception you created as a result of not giving me a chance to communicate with you and this creates misunderstandings of intentions.

This will follow you no matter who you are with because you will always see the worse in them even when that's not the case, I should know.

You made a big thing about some young girl and I was ok with showing you all that I wrote to her, and when you saw what we wrote to each other you realized there was nothing there.

Just as there was nothing there I know I would never cheat on you and I am just as certain that I would have never just decide to use you and throw you away for someone else.

That old man told me that trust is something you must earn. I thought I earned your trust, but what ever I did it was not enough and maybe no matter what anyone does it will never be enough. I hope you will try to take the chance to trust someone one day because it's the only way they can make you happy.

I would never do anything to intentionally hurt you. I don't know why you were so insecure with me and you gave me the feeling that you were always thinking that I would be unfaithful to you. I would never do anything. I would never have been unfaithful to you.

I wish I could have taken you out to nice places and enjoyed the time we spent together going out and doing fun things, but I am a 35-year-old man starting a second career in life in the medical field so I sold everything to finance this goal. I gave you what I could by giving you myself such as bringing you breakfast every morning and hand feeding it to you one bite at a time while you were in the shower as you

rushed for your clinicals and also by doing anything you

asked of me. I don't know what more I could have done. I

don't know what is enough for you. You should spend time

thinking about what are the things that are really important

to you in order to be happy.

Spending time with that old man does not give me the

answers to things, but what he does is help me see the answers

because the answers are all around us. I hope you think

about what I have said because he is a wise old man. So I

said at the beginning I would tell what the old man believes

your greatest fear in life is. Your greatest fear in life is

making the mistake of marrying a man and ending up

divorced with a child to care for because he cheats on you and then leaves you for someone else just as your father did. Not all men are like that. You should not have been so quick to judge me based on a patchwork of bits and pieces of information from my desk or wherever. These things can lead you to see whatever you want in anyone, but instead you should judge people by their actions and how they treated you and by what's in their heart.

I hope you read this carefully and understand the tone is not an attempt to get you to reconcile our relationship because you have made it very clear that you do not want to be with me no matter how just or unjust those reasons are, and I accept that, and besides I don't even know if that's possible now anymore because it is very difficult to undo what has already been done. What I am trying to do is get you to change your ways because I know that has the best chance of leading you to have a relationship with someone else and finding love and happiness. The reason I care is because I love you so much that I am selfless of you and I want to do everything I can to see you happy and in love even if that's with someone else than with me. If that manner of kindness and thoughtfulness is not a good measure of how much someone loves you then I don't know what is, because few people would ever care enough to care about the others future wellbeing after a relationship comes to an end.

I hope you are able to find this happiness one day; it will bring me a tear of joy and one of sorrow. The old man told me to be careful not to let those opportunities of true love slip by because he said they only come by once and maybe twice in a lifetime with on some rare occasions someone gets 3 chances. I think I have just used up my second chance with you, so who knows if I'll ever get a 3rd. Be wise with your time because 10 years will go by in the blink of an eye.

I wish you nothing but all that is good and that you find in life true love and happiness. I hope you have taken the time to read this, but somehow I think you will disregard everything and not even bother to read it and just throw it away in the garbage. Maybe that's where it is supposed to end up for someone else or some other effect that I cannot foresee,

like the "butterfly effect": the idea that the flittering of a

butterfly's wings could be what starts a tsunami thousands of

miles away. I know I have done my part by writing this to you

and doing what is kind and thoughtful and just.

I love you,

R

I always do the right thing; I would have never done

you wrong, you are giving up a good man

I have been writing this at the old mans place since

the beginning of the Sabbath in candle light only since it is all that he will allow, from sunset until tomorrow morning, in mourning for his beloved wife. It's just a Friday night, but it's the kind thing to do and the right thing to do for someone. I will be bringing him tea in a little while. I still haven't decided if I should give this to you. I will be gone by the time you read this tomorrow to do volunteer work overseas for Doctors Without Borders. If you care I will leave you something at the beach cottage.

What is Done is Done

After I was done writing the letter, I thought perhaps whatever I have written must be a horrible jumbled mess of the rambling thoughts of a tortured soul. Then, as I slowly began reading it I realized how much of my heart hung on every word and my hands started to tremble when a teardrop ran down my nose and leaped off and found its place amongst the words, on the word love, smudging it slightly.

What is Done is Done

That teardrop was special, and I wondered if as it was falling it somehow knew there was a place it needed to be from the moment it was born in my eyes. Never in my life have I written anything like this, so something must have been happening for all those coincidences to fall into place and inspire me to create this.

Everything I wrote to her was the truth, but I feared that she would consider me to be like all the other men she has ever known that have lied to her and betrayed her trust. Once in a while someone might come along that deserves a second chance at proving his or her sincerity. It was my hope that she would take that chance with me.

Would she or anybody for that matter care to read it? The possibility crossed my mind that perhaps this is more for me then for her. Might this all be my way of coping and in doing so it would only be for my own peace of mind as a way of sorting out my thoughts in order to move on with my life?

It was a quiet night with only the sound of the ticking clock in the room as could see the clock on the wall over my shoulder on a rustic oval mirror on the wall with sunflowers carved along its frame. I heard a gurgling cough from the bedroom and I knew he had awoken from his nap. I then made him some fresh tea and brought it to him.

When I walked in he was holding a picture frame and was slumped over just staring at it with his fingertips on the glass as if he was touching her. His gazing stare was as endless as mine, when I once stared into the candlelight as I wrote the letter.

Then a whistle from a train shattered the night's silence, as it passed by on the other side of the bay it could be heard in the distance getting closer. When I placed the tea tray on the bed he grabbed my wrist with trembling hands and then his eyes became visible in the light and I saw that they were swelling with tears.

With a perceptive, but shaky voice he turned to me, "I know you are hurting and I know there is some place you must be or something you must do." At that moment, he told me of how at onetime in his life, long ago when he was young he was in my shoes and in the end time will unfold itself, as it should.

It was as if I was talking to myself because when I asked him how he knew of the letter he said, "Because once when I was young I wrote a letter to my wife telling her I loved her, and I feel and see your pain in your eyes just as you do in mine." My future was just beginning to unfold in my hands and I had the power to change it, just as she had the power to change it. The only questioned that remained was, if she stilled loved me. He knew I was leaving tomorrow and as I turned to walkout of the room he told me that if I didn't go I would never know and be left to wonder for the rest of my life asking myself "What if?"

It was some distance away, but when I finally got to her place, I thought I would simply be able to walk up to the door and just slip it under. Far more intimidating then I thought, it stood like a daunting insurmountable barrier as I could see the front door from afar. There it stood almost as if it had a force that pushed me back, that held me at bay as I just leaned up against a tree where we carved our initials. Then with the realization that it may be the last time I ever see this tree again in my life, I started to trace the letters with the tip of my finger just as I would sometimes part her hair away from her eyes when I made love to her. The sensations seemed so real I could just feel the softness of her skin. One day I may feel it again, but for him, he will never be able to feel it again.

Undecided and anxious as I was, I decide to turn away and forget the whole thing, but at that moment I felt her cat rub his nose on my ankles. This was a soothing feeling that calmed and relived me of my fears and doubts if it was worth trying.

Surely, I am not the only one that has ever stood at a fork road in time where regardless of the decision that is made they will all herald a profound ripple of changes into the future from a singularity in time. The thought of always wondering about what would have happened, if I had taken the other road would have lingered and haunted me for the rest of my life. In doing so, at least I know I tried.

One deep breath, and I overcame my anxiety and trepidation, so I just marched right up to the door and slipped it under and at that moment it was too late, even if I wanted to change my mind. My stomach turned with doubt and regret in a sea of an endless sense of restlessness and anticipation at what might happen. What is done is done, and what I set into motion now cannot be stopped. There was no hope of me ever crawling out of this abyss of despair, for I was in so deep now that I questioned if all that was around me was real.

The journey home brought time to a stand still and seemed as if it was going to take the rest of the night to get there. Sweet memories were all that I had of her and they were endlessly playing themselves over and over in my mind. I needed her to feel what I was feeling so she could save me from another endless night of my bleeding heart, if only she knew, if only she could feel what was ravaging my soul from the inside. My eyes flooded with a prism of tears as they warped the city lights into a kaleidoscope.

Maybe she will read her own love story or perhaps she will just remain a bystander in this calamity that I have created and brought upon myself. Regardless within me there was an overwhelming feeling of insatiable curiosity and the need to look out into the future beyond the point where we believe we can predict events. This is all in a vain effort to conceive the possibility that maybe somewhere out there was a horizon of cascading events that will lead to true love that is impossible to foresee.

When I opened the door at my place, it seemed almost empty and devoid of life and knowing she was not there created a cold fog of emotions that only I could see or feel. The room was so quiet that I could hear a faint humming sound of silence from within my ears, as I so missed the sweet sound of her voice. It was too much to bear such silent misery, so I turned on the fan to preoccupy my senses. Lying in bed with the whisper of the fan, I thought if I was the only one that read it, then it might be as if it never happened and it would be forever forgotten in the horizons of time.

Maybe all these thoughts and emotions that are overwhelming me should be shared regardless if she ever reads it. Years may pass before I may ever know anything else beyond the moment when I slip it under her door and begin to walk away. In a strange twist of fate, she may one day be standing or walking beside someone who has read her love story without her even knowing it.

There as I lay in bed, there was a hunger within me that I could feel weighing me down that could not be satisfied with anything but her love. Then just as I was falling asleep, I reached over and clutched her red pillow and held it close. Caressing the pillow lightly with my fingertips I could almost feel the softness and warmth of her skin. My eyes grew heavy in the dim light as I could still sense the faint scent of her soft blond hair on the pillow. Those dreams of mine would bring me into her arms to a timeless place where I could caress her cheek and run my fingers through her hair and kiss her for the first time, as I would then make love to her for the first time. It was all in my dreams now, where it may remain forever.

First

Unforgettable as it was, I will always be able to envision in my dreams the first time I saw her on that special day. When she passed by me in the hall at the hospital it was a blur, as I could barely get a glimpse of her in her white uniform, but my only thought was, "Who was that blond nurse?" With each passing day I could not wait to get a chance to see her again and each time it seemed to last a little longer. This charade of trying to anticipate when I would see her again served only to tease me and taunt my endless desires for more of her.

First

Finally one day I saw her sitting by herself in the cafeteria, so I sat in front of her hoping that it would lead to a conversation. The tension was high because I was shy and didn't want our eyes to engage in a locking glance so I pretended to be studying with a book, which I was pretending to read while I often looked off to the side, as people would walk by. Doubtful at the possibility of her being interested, I was dismissive of the possibility because she was much younger then I, in addition to the fact that she was just starting her medical career, as I was.

Engraved in my mind it will be, I will always remember the first time I looked into her eyes and I fantasized about what it would be like to wake up in the morning and be the first thing I see. I love her so much I miss her eyes when she blinks, but she may never come to know these feelings I have for her, because I have been so scarred in the past and have had my heart ripped out of my chest and handed to me. Wearing a mask to hide my feelings and emotions because I feared being hurt made it very difficult to express my true feelings for her, but this is something I hoped to overcome with time, if she was patient with me.

Those lips of hers seemed so rosy and soft, and then that sweet smile with an adorable little gap between her front teeth was what did it for me, because I saw there was beauty in her diminutive imperfections. Impossible as it was, I could not resist wondering what they would feel like if my lips touched hers. They were begging me almost eagerly and I wondered if I would even be able to keep my eyes open as I kissed her or would they overcome my senses and demand of my subconscious that my eyes surrender and only focus on her lips. What a dilemma!

Seemingly, it was almost as if I had the ears of some animal, because by only knowing that she was wearing white nylons under her nurse's uniform, in my mind I could practically hear the rubbing sounds as they pressed against the uniform on top. Then my mind wondered to the border where the nylons stop and her soft creamy skin begin, as I thought they were something only a blind man could appreciate. Down from a whirlwind of desire for her it all suddenly came to an end, because she needed to get back to her patients. She reached forward and her small hand touched mine in a handshake that like an alarm clock, it served to snap me out of the delusional fantasy I was in. To this day I am not sure what we talked about, as I must have somehow been lucidly coherent enough to carry on a conversation with her.

Over time as luck would have it, our chance meetings in the halls became more frequent and our exchange of smiles more memorable with each passing moment as our paths crossed. People might notice and I was starting to get worried, because what if things are not as I perceived them and she was just being herself. Doubts continued to resurface in my mind, if she really was thinking of me the way I was dreaming of her. My doubts were soon erased when she left me a note in my locker telling me, "I think you're cute." I remember those words must have shorted out my vagus nerve as my heart felt like it was going to jump out and run down the halls knocking on patients doors.

The feeling of her love and affection for the first time was so blissful. Maybe it had been about ten years since I felt that way about anyone, ever since I was 22 years old and I met my second girlfriend in my life, so she was the first true love in my life. At the time I was too young and I lacked direction in my life and she was 7 years older then I with an unmerciful biological clock that was ticking away. Caught by surprise, I did not think I would ever feel that way about anyone again until I met this beautiful blond nurse and turned my life upside-down.

One day she asked me in a very casual way, by just mentioning that she worked at a diner just a few blocks away as a waitress to pay her way through nursing school. She suggested that I stop by for a cup of coffee sometime and then she added that she got off at eleven. Going beyond just thinking I was cute and flirting with me, I thought this must surely be a sign she was clearly interested in me as more than a casual friend.

That night, I walked into the diner with some time to spare so there would be no rush for what I had planed. Instantly from the other side of the diner she noticed me as soon as I walked in, as she paused briefly while taking a customers order she glanced over long enough to lose her thoughts. With some embarrassment she asked the customer to kindly repeat their order, all while fighting a losing battle not to smile at me.

First

It wasn't long before she came over and had me seated at the back by the swinging double doors to the kitchen. As soon as I sat down, I kicked back with my hands behind my head and fingers interlocked. Leaning back against the wall there was no place in the diner where I could not gaze upon her like a child's candy fantasy, all while fighting my own losing battle not to succumb to her passing smile each time she glanced over.

With amazement I watched, as she walked back and forth among the tables in a very plain black skirt barely above the knee with black nylons and a checkered black and white short sleeve shirt, which outlined her curves so very closely. In my mind she was putting on a show for me like a ballerina in a jewelry box with the diner as her stage. All the while, a song on the jukebox crooned to the room with a soft ballad that was so befitting the moment that I knew I would always remember that moment every time I heard that song for the rest of my life.

Like a tornado she came over and told me she was done and just needed a minute to change in the bathroom. I was just wearing blue jeans and a black t-shirt for casual comfort. My first thought was she was going to be gone much longer, but suddenly she swung the bathroom door open and said, "Lets go" as she put on her shoes. That moment was long enough for me to notice every curve on her body with the red tang top she was wearing, and then my eyes wondered down to her bare legs in a short jean skirt. Like everything else about her, they were on the one hand mesmerizing and on the other they could wake the dead.

Not wanting to spoil the surprise, I told her I had something special in mind, a really fancy place where we could go and be served some very fine cuisine with the most spectacular views in the city. By the time I finished she had a very angry expression and snapped back with, "Have you noticed the way I'm dressed." I chuckled to ease the tension and insisted that she should just relax and look at the way I was dressed, and besides I know the chef personally. That frown of hers faded away although almost regrettably, because I thought she looked so adorable with a drop of anger, being that it was an expression on her that I had never seen. Almost as if she was that ballerina doll come to life, and I could not help to wonder in amazement at what else this beautiful doll of mine could do.

First

On the way over to our destination, I was taunted by the subliminal flashing from the city lights on her seat illuminating her soft feminine curves. Once there I leaned into her so closely I could feel her breathing upon my ear, as I reached into the backseat and grabbed a small basket. Just as I leaned back and I pulled it over towards me, I saw an eager and devilish smile biting down on her lips with that delightful little slit between her front teeth. I looked at her with a smile, "I told you I knew the chef, I hope you like my burgers, but I'm sure you will enjoy the champagne."

We walked past all the neon lights where the herds of people gathered until we reached a small coral stonewall standing just below the waist. With one step I stood on top of it and extended my hand to her, my palms were just as moist as hers. The sea grass danced in the ocean wind on the sand dune ahead of us, as if charmed by the melody of that soft ballad echoing in my mind. I could still hear it and I think she could hear it too. As we crossed the sand dune, the neon lights and the sounds of the herd faded away behind us. We had all that we needed to run away from it all in that basket without ever looking back and lose ourselves in each other.

The minutes turned to hours and we talked about everything and anything from childhood memories to our future dreams and the life there after. We quenched our thirst and our hunger, all but for each other. In the dim light of the moon, the aura of light from our lantern streaked shadows of her hair across her face as they swayed in the wind up and over her lips. A moment came when it seemed there was nothing else to say as we looked into each other's eyes in silence. Few words were needed as I asked her to close her eyes, and then from under a small white towel in the basket I presented her with a rose when she opened them.

With that blinding passionate smile of hers, she touched the rose with her nose as it covered her lips and she lightly kissed the rose as she looked into my eyes while blowing me a kiss. Then she stood up and led me with a gentle tug of my hand to walk with her. Our bare feet sank into the wet sand with each step as the small waves broke and the white water blanketed them. Leading each other hand by hand, before we realized it we were at our knees in the white water. I looked into her eyes and my hand gently caressed her cheek.

First

Suddenly, she then turned her back to me and I caressed her from behind tracing her naval with the tip of my finger, while my other hand caressed her cheek slowly down the side of her neck as she tilted her head to one side. I could feel her pulse and then she felt my lips kiss her softly beside my fingertips. I whispered into her ear, "Let me be yours," and she turned around in my arms, then as I looked into her eyes, I closed mine in sweet surrender to her lips.

In my arms she quivered sending ripples carried away by the whitewater to the ends of the earth for generations to come. It was a moment frozen in time that would last us forever. Destined to repeat history for eternity in my dreams in the horizons of time I would always be forever young thinking of her.

That Day

That day before dusk as I anxiously awaited her, she knocked on the door and I saw that smile of hers with such passion that it blinded me like rays of light and forced my eyes to capitulate to her lips as I looked into her eyes and closed them.

My place was just a modest and simple little beach cottage in back of a large house. It was a cozy little place with only the bare essentials, just one bedroom and a bathroom with a single stove. When the owners are away up North, which is most of the time, I would watch over the place.

With the ocean beckoning us for appreciation we went for a walk on the beach with her dog Bruno, a large old German Shepard, but with enough frisk to still frolic with the seagulls. While holding hands and sharing each other's future dreams we walked until the sun foretold us of its setting with longer casting shadows. I told her of my dream to one day join Doctors Without Borders and live in Israel or a Slavic country in the Mediterranean, while seasonally helping to provide medical care for people in Africa that are so poor they are not even wearing shoes.

The gratitude I would get from the people I helped along with some pictures of the harsh realities of the surroundings with the contrasting glimmers of joy and hope, would at the very least make for a tantalizing personalized photo album on a coffee table, as well as for some epic story telling one day. Surprisingly, she agreed to follow me to those distant lands on my journey and work along side of me, with the caveat that one day we call home some small island across many bridges in a southern state. It was a compromise that I could live with, mile marker zero.

With sand still stuck between our toes while leaving a trail we entered the cottage and we laid out on the carpet with our furry friend beside us. While she rubbed his tummy, the story of her life began to unfold, as she told me about her childhood and having lived in the Midwest for a short while, until she ended up living in the Southeast. There was a large loving family awaiting her at home, her mother and stepfather who she proudly proclaimed, "Was the only man she knew that looked manly with a glass of wine in his hand." In the future she would never find herself alone because she was the eldest of four younger sisters. If she only knew how fortunate I thought she was, because I had no brothers or sisters and all that remained of my family was my mother and my aunt, and unavoidably that would one day leave me without anyone. If only she were to fall in love with me, I would not be left without a family and endless searching in distant lands for belongingness and solace in the horizons of time.

The day was coming to an end, as I offered her something to eat and while I prepared something for us, she wandered about the room occasional looking over at me as I stood by the stove, almost as if seeking approval before reaching out to touch something. When I brought the food over to her, there was a photo album that she had removed from a shelf and placed on the bed. It was as if she would not dare open it, but I peaked her curiosity when I told her they were baby pictures of me. Those curious eyes of hers spun with delight as her eyebrows ran away.

We embarked on a journey through my past, as we began the march well stocked enough to feed an army, while we sat Indian style on the bed facing each other with the album between us. They started to recount a bedtime story with each turning of the page. When she saw what I looked like back in high school she only wished that she had known me back then. Then, there I was as a child playing amongst toys in a seemingly imaginary world of stuffed animals. She cooed over me, all dressed in white as I took my First Communion. With the bubbly eruption of a giggle and a silly smile she was blasted away by a baby boy bouncing on his father's knees with his mother standing by, as she seemingly lost her balance only to catch herself on my shoulder.

At the turn of the final page was a baby boy lying in a crib in his birthday suit and it was the only photo she remained silent for.

The light was wearing thin and Bruno was at the foot of the bed lying on the rug. Then as I reached over to one of the lamps on the nightstand, and my hand approached, she tackled my arm with both of her hands and was quickly followed by her whisper, "Don't." With longing eyes that blinked ever so slowly, she humbly tilted her head. In the fleeting light I could see she was fervently biting her lower lip.

With a soft smile, I stared into her eyes then gently broke free of her grasp and reached into the drawer. In the dark I struck a match to light the scented candle, and just then I could hear a playful laugh behind me.

The candles flame fluttered in the ocean breeze, as the curtains swayed open and closed parting and descending as if we were on a theater stage between acts or at the end of a stupendous performance. In the swirls of the wind the candles mulberry medley potpourri aroma permeated the room and warmed our souls. With an overwhelming applause of an opening act from the ocean waves breaking in the distance, my eyes were at long last victorious as I kissed her lips while looking into her eyes. In the candlelight we painted the walls with our shadows, there was no shadow that remained untouched or unexplored neither by hand nor by shadow.

There was nothing else in the world I could want with this Greek girl of mine resting her head on my shoulder, and as our eyes grew heavy I told her that I loved her. Like a Greek myth, I was her Pyramus and she was my maiden Thisbe. Concealing our emotions from others as we pass by each other in the hallways of the hospital only able to express our emotions by passing glances or subtle signs. One day, we escaped those walls to meet by the burning candlelight of the Mulberry tree. Thousands of years ago their love for each other stained the fruit of the Mulberry tree deep purple and the commingling of our love has bestowed the sweet scent of its fruit.

A princes in the morning as I would do always, I awoke before her and kissed her delicately on her forehead, so as to not arouse her from her sleep. When she opened her eyes, I had already made her breakfast and neatly laid out her nursing uniform and polished her white shoes for those adorable dainty feet that she dismissed as ugly, but to me nothing about her was unsightly. In the mad rush of the morning, while she got dressed I made her lunch and packed it for her in a bag, as I watched her from the stove and regrettably wished she could stay in my arms all day long while I caress her.

In seclusion and completely cutting myself off from the rest of the world, after she would leave I would unbeknownst to her begin to write stories in my writers manuscript, encompassing all my thoughts of her and of our time spent together which served as my inspiration. One day, I envisioned pursuing my secret love of writing and photojournalism of distant lands, but I never fathomed writing a poetic love story of my life. For every word is accompanied by a tear born of inspiration like drops of nectar from the Mulberry tree.

Drops of Nectar

Nervous as I was, I knew I would probably be meeting her stepfather who she called dad, and her mother for the first time that day. Once I arrived at her house, I hesitated before knocking and wondered what they would be saying to each other about me after I met them.

Would her father be satisfied with the way I shake his hand? Maybe it's just something men think about, because as a man I knew how important it is to make a good impression with that first handshake. You can tell a lot about someone by the way they shake hands, so it has to be just right and not be too strong or last too long and always following the lead of the hand who is dominant in a given scenario. Certainly his hand was dominant as that was his house and I needed to show respect.

Mothers hope their daughters will find someone that will love them and make them happy and for which they can picture her beside him in a tuxedo with her dressed in white. Picturesque as in a fairy tale of a knight in shining armor, a true gentleman the kind that would bow and kiss their princess hand. I needed to live up to that dream and be that knight in shining armor to prove myself worthy of their daughters love.

Greeting me as I stood at the front door, her cat rubbed his nose against my ankles and served to distract me and relive some of my anxiety. Instantly we became friends as I tickled him under his chin while he purred. In jest I thought, if only it were that easy after I knock on the door.

Suddenly, the door opened as they saw someone from the inside at the front door. It was her mother and I greeted her with a light, but very warm and loving hug as our cheeks barely touched. Out of nowhere her younger sisters came running as they enthusiastically showed me their new litter of kittens. Mothers have perceptive senses for feelings, so I hoped that she could feel the love for her daughter radiating from my soul.

Rising up from a sofa at the back of the room, her father a six-foot tall Italian walked over to greet me. Those were some of the longest seconds in my life, as it felt like it was happening in slow motion. With a firm, but confident handshake and good eye contact followed by a receptive and friendly smile, I just might have managed to pull it off.

Breathing a little easier after it was all over; I thought maybe I made the impression I so desperately hoped for. Bearing a sport fishermen's tan, her dad was the kind of guy I could enjoy having a beer with while we troll for big game fish. Authoritative as a drill sergeant running a tight shift, her mother was a no nonsense tuff love supermom that juggled life with four young daughters and ran a household that I would imaging at times she thought were a zoo from everything going on at the same time.

That day we had made plans that I would take her on lovely excursion through the natural wonders of a nearby park. Every step we took created new memories born with the tenacity to embed themselves deep in our minds to last a lifetime. The park was just an hour away and thrived with a wondrous variety of wild life. Bruno waged his tail with the excitement of puppy going for his first walk. Even as she merely walked with Bruno by her side, I found it momentous enough to begin taking pictures of her, of them.

On a dilapidated wooden pier at the edge of the mangroves we got a canoe for a few hours. Traveling in a calm slow moving creek surrounded by mangroves and surrounded by the beauty of nature was humbling to see what life has to offer. She told me how badly she wanted to have a girl one day, and I agreed as long I could teach her to play baseball with a glove that I have been saving that's just big enough to fit a child's hand. It was my glove a long time ago and I wanted to share it with my first child regardless if it's a boy or a girl. I took pictures as she made exaggerated poses for the camera while wearing a beach hat and sunglasses and with Bruno's head popping up in the middle now and again.

The charm of a modest island lay in the distance and drew our curiosity as to what secrets or adventures it may hold. Almost as if in search of a secrete treasure we disembarked with the eagerness of explorers searching for the fountain of youth.

She picked up a stick on the shore and threw it as far as she could as Bruno chased after it and the ducks by the water. I went on a quest deep into the mangroves on the high roots exposed above the waterline.

There was a shallow pool of water with leaves spruced across the surface where the light from the sun found its way threw even the soaring meanderings of the tree branches and gave the pool of water a golden reflection. I called out for her to come, so I could share this natural beauty with her. We were both entranced by the miraculous allure of this natural wonder that only we knew about.

The moment we emerged from the thick mangroves I saw Bruno swimming a few feet from the shoreline, but then I noticed he was thrashing. I dropped my camera as I ran to him into the waist deep water and garbed him from behind and helped him over the top of the mangrove branches under the water that were blocking him from reaching the shore. He swam the last few feet to shore and I slowly waded back trying to catch my breath.

When she started running behind me she twisted and sprained her ankle on the rocky shoreline. Limping on one leg she hugged Bruno and cried. It was only then that I noticed that she was hysterical on an emotional rollercoaster after having almost lost her best friend on four paws.

When we returned to the dock, there was an elderly couple feeding the birds on a bench and she turned to me with a smile, "That could be us someday." We could both see the man on the bench was much older then his wife, so I asked her if she was certain that she would prefer to be with me then a younger man, but she quickly reassured me that her preference was for a mature man that she could feel secure with.

Sitting at the edge of the dock with our legs dangling over the edge, I offered to create something for her from nothing. In my pocket was a one-inch folding scissor and four small pieces of paper, one orange, yellow, green and pink. The puzzled and mysterious look on her face grew, as I urged her to wait and see and to be patient. Carefully I folded and cut thin little slices and segments from each of the four colors as I carefully crafted them together. Soon she realized what it was, that I created for her out of almost nothing. My creation for her was a raised three-dimensional flower. Should she decide to be with me, I knew we could create anything we dreamed of from nothing as long as we had each other.

There would never be a day when I would grow old as long as I was with her or thinking of her. In my mind she would always be the same as the day I met her, because by loving her I discovered the fountain of youth. If she would go blind I would be her eyes and see for her, and if she could not walk I would be her legs. I would care and protect her from the stormy seas of the horizons of time until my last breath. We had created a day filled with memories from the simplest of things and a profound appreciation for one another.

Drops of Nectar

Over the next few days Bruno became more lethargic as his heart grew older and weaker with each beat. Without hesitation, in her time of need I helped her care for him and together in his time of need we cared for our furry friend. Then one day we said goodbye to Bruno, and I was by her side as she held his paw and then I hugged her when it went limp. My cheek was wet from her tears as it pressed against hers as I hugged her ever so tightly that I could feel her breathing. I would always be there for her in life to wipe away her tears whenever she cried and I would replace them with the joy and the love I have for her.

Upon arriving at her home one day, I heard the faint sounds of a crying puppy from under her front door. When she opened the door it was a little baby Bruno zipping around the room as he waged his tail and chewed on anything he could get in his mouth from the furniture to the curtains.

Earlier that day, feeling lonely without Bruno by her side she went to a local veterinarians clinic where they were giving him away to anyone who wanted to love him and give him a good home. That was one lucky dog, as a loving and caring family would surround him

for the rest of his life, if only I were that lucky.

Green Eye

During that summer, every night I massaged her ankle as I cared for her every whimper and ache. I lovingly nursed her back to health, as all she needed was rest and time to heal. Patiently I sat outside her doctor's office while her ankle was examined and x-rayed. To prevent her from straining her ankle, I helped her in getting to her nursing school classes every morning and I returned punctually afterwards to take her home. There was no shortcoming need of hers that I did not meet, because whatever she could not do I was there to do it for her.

Green Eye

Sometimes in the middle of the night the swelling and aching pain in her ankle were such that she could not fall asleep and I would then go to the store for her prescriptions. Upon my return I would surprise her with a treat for her sweet tooth, to satisfy her nocturnal craving for her favorite ice cream. In sickness and in health, it was as if she was my baby to love and to hold and to care for her, for as long as could. Then I would massage her ankle, and as she would fall asleep and without her knowing, I would then cover her with my blanket to keep her warm at night, followed by lightly kissing her on the forehead to not arouse her from her sleep.

Then when her ankle healed and summer faded and the nights grew colder, I walked into the diner late one night after finishing up at the hospital in hopes of seeing her there. There was a very young waitress just starting her first year of college that smiled at me and blushed, incapable of bringing herself to look me in the eye, while shyly lusting in secret. Hastily she seated me at the entrance of the diner, right by where she greeted other patrons as they walked in. While I waited for my love to arrive the young waitress offered to serve me coffee, "On the house," she said, "Because you work at the hospital."

Over time with each visit to the diner for coffee we became friends and shared our jokes and gripes of the day. Caution prevailed, because I did not want anyone to get the impression there was anything between us and I was well aware that she was just a teenager infatuated with an older man. Despite telling her that my heart was already committed to someone, she persisted and regrettably my efforts to discourage her advances were not persuasive enough for her to end her flirting. However things may have appeared, there should be no doubt that I was always faithful and true to my fiancé, as I would have always been forever.

Then, on a rainy night I was tied up later then usual during my clinicals with patients, so my timing was off and I arrived at the diner later then I would have liked. The young waitress greeted me with her usual bubbly joy, but there was a hint of sadness and worry that weighed down her typical glee. It was then, that she told me of her worries regarding her mother's response to medical treatments she was undergoing.

Green Eye

Fortunately, I was friends with several doctors at the hospital and I suggested she seek a second opinion, as I gave her a specialist's card. It was a slow night, so she sat down with me and we then began talking about her life as she painted a picture of her life long ambitions of one day becoming a veterinarian, an equine specialist. There were such wonderful stores she had of summers in the bay fishing with her brothers and her father. It was as if she lived without a care in the world. Yes, she was a happy go lucky girl.

Our momentum was broken by the sound of a ringing telephone at the counter. The cook from behind the counter called out to her with the phone in one hand and a spatula in the other. Almost from the moment she picked it up there was a frantic and desperate look on her face and she dashed out the door into the rain.

Out of concern for my friend, I ran after her and it was then she told me her mother was in the hospital. In the rain, out sympathy and compassion for her I offered her my raincoat and I walked with her to the hospital just up the street. That night, she cried by her mothers bedside and I consoled her emotional needs until she fell asleep in a chair while she held her mothers hand. During the night, before leaving I covered her with a blanket and turned off the lights.

In the coming days, she would send me several emotional cards expressing her feelings of gratitude and appreciation, but always with a hint of something more. There was never an instance in all of my replies suggesting any romantic feelings for her, as I always wished her well as a friend and reinforced my commitment to my fiancé.

On a Sunday afternoon after a siesta, she awoke before me and found the empty envelopes with the young waitress name on them. The furry in the room awoke me from my sleep and I could see her eyes were green and fuming with jealousy. Without a trial she quickly jumped to conclusions about me that had no basis in fact. The accusations were thrown at me as in stoning execution.

In between the flinging stones, I managed to make my way crawling over to desperately reach the desk drawer where inside beside my writers manuscript were the letters in their entirety. Crying out for mercy, I urged and appealed for her to read them before continuing the unjust execution of my love for her.

Green Eye

There was no doubt left in her, after the startling realization from reading them that I was innocent of all that she accused me of, because I was always loyal to her as she concluded there was not a shred to be found of an improper nature. All she needed to do, and what she should have done was to just ask me about her and I would have given her all the letters for her to read. No temptress could ever compel me to betray my true love. If only she knew this, but her heart had been battered and scared from past relationships and the infidelity of those she trusted with her heart. This was a burden I would be forced to carry, but I didn't know how long I would be able to even if I wanted to continue to endure her suspicions of me.

Trust is something that must be earned, and my belief that I had done all I could to have already earned her trust was shattered, and I was left feeling bruised and bloodied as if she really didn't know the kind of man I am. There was nothing more I wanted at that moment as I was left there on my knees yearning for her sweet embrace and to hear the lasting words "I love you." Those could have the power to heal my love for her and make me whole again. Then, as if no stone had ever been cast she just went about as if nothing had happened.

Wishing for her to trust me, I was left to wonder if she ever would or if she ever did at all.

There I was, a man that stood before her knowing that I would never betray her and would never do anything to hurt her, but it was almost as if she could not allow herself to believe that she had found what she had been searching for all her life. The others in her life before me set the president of mistrust that would forever haunt her and her relationship with me.

Once in a while we are handed a gift by mere chance. I was her new gift that she could open everyday for the rest of her life and I would give her joy and happiness again and again, as I delicately and tenderly caress her. Every word I spoke to her has always carried my thoughtful kindness and love for her, not once have I ever degraded her in a derogatory way or mistreated her as my hands always touched her softly and gently. Whatever she feels, I feel and my bones ache at the thought of her pain. There was no place I would rather be then in her arms, for my heart was committed to bringing her joy in life.

Green Eye

Trust is the keystone of a relationship, and ours was beginning to splinter and fester. Without hesitation or any reservations in my mind, I trusted her unconditionally with my life, however she doubted me where there should never have been any doubt. Feeling as if no matter what I did she would never let go of the hurt from her past and trust me without holding back, I then pondered and then wept at the thought of living without her love.

Those who dare yonder to a dream of loving without holding back, without any reservations can be a perilous endeavor that can break ones heart, but without doing so one will never know the meaning or for that matter the feeling of true intimacy, true joy, and true love.

The Storm

Thoughtful of her as always, and taking the care of not waking her from the deep sleep of a Sunday morning, I quietly slipped out on an errand to the store so I can make her something tasty to eat, for the both of us to enjoy breakfast together. Running this errand took me significantly longer then usual, because it was raining so much that I decided to wait at the store until it was just a drizzle. There was a break in the storm that I was waiting for, and I took advantage of it and hurried back to the cottage before the rains would return.

The Storm

To my surprise upon entering the room, I saw she had awoken and I noticed she was reading one of her medical textbooks at my desk. This was not unusual and I thought nothing of it, so I began unpacking the bags of food and putting them away. Next, just as I asked her if she wanted something to eat, she gave me a snappy reply, but I just brushed it off. Then, I asked if she wanted any juice with the cereal and this time it was followed by a senseless argument over the number of calories per serving in the juice. It was something so frivolous that I came to my senses after about just a minute or two of arguing and I simply told her she was right. Now thinking that would be the end, it only enraged her even more and she bolted straight to the bathroom with a stomping march that shook the wooden floor as she slammed the door.

There I was left wondering, "What was happening?" From the time she woke up, to breakfast something must have happened. This enigma was something I just could not figure out. There I was left wondering, how it was possible that I could have played a role in her rage, whatever it was based on.

After what must have been at least an hour in the bathroom she emerged, however this time much calmer and collected. I was thinking that everything was fine, but she sits down on the couch next to me and tells me she has decided to go home early that weekend, instead of staying until Monday. This was very unusual, because typically she would stay until Monday and it was obvious that she had originally intended to stay the entire weekend.

Now I was not just really puzzled, but I was shocked at how far it was all going to go. Although I tried to convince her to stay it was useless, even as I told her how much I loved her, but that was just useless and seemingly meant nothing to her. Strangely enough, she acted as though it was nothing to worry about because she gave me a long goodbye kiss as she usually did.

Days passed and she grew colder and more distant whenever she would talk to me, as if there was something else more important for her to do. Later in the week, instead of making plans to come over the following weekend she was coordinating with me for a convenient time when she could get some of her things that were left behind at the cottage.

The Storm

This was all too overwhelming for me, because I could not understand what was wrong. I need to know once and for all where things stood, so I simply asked her, "Do you still want to be with me?" and "What did I do?"

Every answer to my questions was vague and was circular in logic, "I can't be with you because I can't make you happy," and "You need someone that can make you happy and I can't do that." There was never a clear answer for why, especially given how sudden things changed.

Regardless of sparing no effort in my attempts at trying to get a clear answer out of her, it was useless and eventually I gave up trying. Over the next few days, I collected and gave her everything she had left behind at the cottage. Then, over the next few days she completely stopped talking to me.

One night, as I was pondering at my desk in the cottage and torturing myself as I brainstormed for the answer as to what could have happened, I noticed the answer might have been in front of me all along. There in front of me, where she was reading her textbook when

I walked in to the cottage was the answer. At my desk, I looked down at my drawer where I store my writer's manuscript and I started to think.

My writer's manuscript contains some fact, but it is also filled with fictional characters and situations and newspaper clippings as well as stories friends send me and I in turn forward to other friends, and for the most part has very little if any basis on reality or my life for that matter. Then I thought, "Is it possible that she may have read my writers manuscript and thought it was some sort of diary or personal journal as it relates to my life?"

That couldn't be it, because everyone knows that a writer's manuscript can often contain a hodgepodge of all sorts of writings, right? Yet, it would have been easy for her to have just asked to see the waitress's thank you letters and my replies, but she didn't and instead jumped to conclusions about me that were very mistaken.

How likely was it, that she read the manuscript and confused fiction for fact and that baseless conclusions about me were reached with regards to what was contained in my writer's manuscript? I suppose it's possible, because as an aspiring writer I have in the past had an interest in researching and writing about bizarre and esoteric topics from a variety of themes and storylines. Its uncertain what she may have thought, but I didn't take my writing seriously because it was something that was not based on reality.

In my stories I always write about women in scenes of passion from my memories, so because all three of the women in my past had dark hair, it was what I could imagine most vividly in my mind. The first blond in my life was her, and the first time I made love to her I was in some disbelief, as she told me that I was the only man she had ever been with that was able to find that place inside of her and make her feel the ecstasy of being a woman, which she had never felt before. Since she was just twenty-five years old, it was plausible that nobody had ever been able to please her. The women in my past were all much older, five, seven, and ten years older then I was, and I was with each of them for several years. Maybe without realizing it, an older woman's experience was something that became a part of me.

This was my first time with a younger woman as well as my first time with a blond. When I met her, it had been three years since my last girlfriend and at the time coincided with the decision to begin a career in the medical field, because the dedication of time needed to pursue such an ambitious goal can be very difficult on a relationship. Since then, I hardly gave myself time to think of relationships.

The first time I made love to her, I fulfilled all her needs as never before and she was able to please me, as it had been so long since I felt a woman's touch. Over time, although I was able to please her there were often times were she could not satisfy me completely. There were times when she asked me, if I was having an affair with someone, and I assured her that I was not because it was the truth. Later on, I came to realize that in my mind her mistrust in me broke my feelings of intimacy and her blond hair was a diversion almost as if there was someone else in the room with us. I believe this lead her to feel insecure and inadequate and possibly even guilty for not being able to please me.

Paradoxically, although I was experienced enough to know how to be with a woman and touch her in ways to fulfill all her needs, I was also permeated by the thought of dark hair, because that was all I had ever experienced. Just like Ivan Pavlov's dogs were conditioned to salivate at the sound of a bell if associated with food, I realized that the dark hair of a woman was all I had ever experienced and had over years become a conditioned stimulus. It was her trust in me that I felt was missing and it had taken with it the feeling of intimacy, of being one soul when making love, and so it was not always easy for her to satisfy me completely even though I would have no problem pleasing her.

Any psychologist knows that over time with patience, a conditioned response can become extinct and replaced by thoughts of making love to her with her lovely blond hair. This may be why some men have a preference for blonds or brunets and might answer the question why some men are so passionate when their wife or girlfriend changes their hair color. Is it possible that some men might subconsciously feel as though they are with another woman, where as others may feel awkward?

I know that I could have gotten accustomed to making love to her with her blond hair, all I needed was a little patience without her unfounded suspicions and insecurities of ever being unfaithful to her.

What I needed from her was to trust me again and the patience those older women had for me at a time when I was young and inexperienced and knew nothing, because I was in love with her regardless of her mistrust in me, or her hair color. What I also needed from her, was to help me build lasting memories in my mind of her over time and to make the psychological association of making love to her. To do so, would have made her the only indelible mark of feminine existence in my mind and completely cripple my ability to be with anyone else but her, and thus extinguish all her doubts and fears and insecurities in one swoop.

Maybe knowing why she walked out the door that day is not important anymore, and maybe it doesn't make a difference anymore. Still I wondered, but it was impossible for me to know, because as the weeks went by she no longer talked to me, and even though weeks had gone by she would not even reply to a simple casual hello.

Over the Horizon

On a new morning, the sun rose over the beach and beamed through the windows of the cottage and on to my face, as the orange glow on the inside of my eyelids awoke me.

With her red pillow clutched tightly, I opened my eyes. I experienced blissful dreams of her, from the day I met her to our first kiss, and of us laughing and crying together, I even dreamt of the first time I made love to her and of the day I met her family. I would always dream of her, so long as I would have her pillow by my side as I fall asleep.

It was as if the night before was just a dream, and I was in disbelief that I had actually written the letter and taken the chance of risking the heart ache of knowing if she would ever be with me again. Going on with my life thinking, if I only had done something more, would probably be worse. That was the reason I was able to bring myself to writing her the letter and giving it to her, even though I knew that waiting for a reply if any would be agony.

My bags were all packed, as I was scheduled to leave just after noon that day. I would finally be going to realize the dream of doing volunteer work for people by providing them with medical care they desperately needed. One day, I would eventually be returning to the states, but that seemed like a world away and there was a good chance when I did, that it would be some other state. This is a place where memories of my love for her still haunt me and linger in the dawn of the morning's light and in the shadows at dusk. When I grip her red pillow and hold it close to my face, I could almost delude myself that she was sound asleep with her head resting by my side waiting for me to kiss her gently on the forehead so as to not wake her.

The room seemed cold and empty, as I stood by the door that I was about to close and leave all trace of her behind forever. On a card I wrote, "I'll will always be yours, you know where to find me." Then, I placed her pillow in the center of the bed with a rose and a note of where she could find me in a land far over the horizon. When I closed the door behind me, it seemed to sound almost artificial as if none of this was really happening and I would wakeup from my nightmare.

Three months had gone by, and I was nearing the end of my four-month tour of volunteer work at a remote medical outpost before heading back to the states. The nights were hot and the days were even hotter and my only escape was dreaming of her and hoping that she would at least write to me one day, because not even in my dreams could I realistically believe that she would ever show up there in person.

Late in the afternoon, I would go in my tent for the sake of having time to myself and sit on an uncomfortable foldout cot, and write in my writer's manuscript with the insect netting draped over my head to keep the flies from crawling up my nose. This small personal space was the only place I could find, where I could escape to and write. There was such human misery all around me that I could hear the suffering cries of sick children in the other tents day and night. I was the only American in our medical outpost, so I stuck out like a sore thumb because the others were mostly European and the rest were from South America.

There were several Israelis and I seemed to be able to fit in with them better then I could with the others. We would eat together and share stories with each other of our lives back home and of those we missed. They would always invite me for their readings of the Torah and for the first time in my life, even though I am not religious I discovered my appreciation for its wisdom. We all became such good friends that they invited me to stay with them and their family in Israel after our completion of voluntary service. Spending some time in Israel, and gaining an understanding of Hebrew culture before heading back home to the states was very appealing to me, but it was something that I wished I could share with someone special, unfortunately that someone did not realize how much I loved her.

Everyone in that desolate land had a sad story, as death from disease and famine were common. However, one day an event stood out like no other when a young woman with her three-month-old daughter was brought to us. The woman was out gathering the meager scraps of food she could for her new born, when her leg was mangled from having stepped on a landmine and gangrene was well into its advanced stages with a systemic infection.

The woman knew she was dying and as I walked by her cot she grabbed my arm. She spoke to me; a translator told me she wanted her daughter to remain at the camp with me. We were all won over by the adorable baby girl. There was a special place in my heart for her, as I bottle-feed her every day. When I would hold her, I could not help but thinking if she was here and saw this little girl she would certainly fall in love with this beautiful baby girl and never want to let her go. Maybe things happen for a reason and they are not always obvious to us at the time.

Over the Horizon

Over time friendships grew with my colleagues and as the months past, one late afternoon a French friend walks into my tent with news of the arrival of a new set of volunteers. With a heavily accented English he adds, "You won't be the only Yank around here anymore, there's an American with the new volunteers and it's a woman." More then that was not necessary to peak my curiosity as I got up and tangled myself in the insect netting, and I hurriedly attempted to rush out and have a look for myself.

There were no women among the volunteers when I got there and since then none had arrived. With that in mind, I thought maybe it could be her, but I didn't want to give myself false hope and the reasonable side of my brain told me that I must be crazy to think like that. Losing my mind by thinking of her in a place like that was a top priority on my list of things to avoid at all cost; it was only second to not getting myself killed. That place was miserable and dangerous enough as it was, and I did not want to make it anymore of a hellish place then it already was.

Stepping outside the tent, I could see the embankment leading up to the hill from where we were perched at the campsite. I was barely able to distinguish features, because of the thermal heat waves rising up from the ground over about a half-mile distance blurred them out. As the new volunteers emerged, one by one from the truck in the distance it was impossible to spot the woman in the group, because they were all wearing desert hats, so even their hair color was not visible. Suddenly, one of them removes their hat and waves of blond hair swayed from side to side as she tied it backup up into a pony tail and slipped it back under her hat. Meanwhile my mouth gaped open in surprise, as I squinted in a futile effort to see more. It was about a five-minute hike up that embankment to where our campsite was situated with the backpacks they were carrying, so I would soon know.

Grueling as it was, I could barely keep myself from running down that hill, as if I were in a movie with a symphony of music playing in the background, but I thought its probably not her and then I'll really look like a fool. Questions in my mind begged to be answered. Is it really she, or might it be the start of a chance to find true intimacy, true joy and true love? I don't know if it's her, maybe its just another mirage of true love in the horizons of time.

Over the Horizon

Eluding a vision of a possible future with her, if it really was her presented itself as an impossible feat for my mind to avoid. Knowing her, the adorable baby girl would win her heart and perhaps she may not be able to bring herself to leave that baby behind when it came time to return home. Surprising her with the suggestion, that maybe we could try and get the necessary legal documents to be able to make her ours and take her home with us, would be followed by an expression of joy on her face that I could only see in my dreams. Would my dreams come true, all depended if that was really her walking up that embankment. I would soon know, and be either overwhelmed with joy or grief from a shattered fantasy for a possible future life.

When bringing love to an end, one should be very certain there is no reasonable doubt of innocence and committing a travesty of love. It is unknown how many chances in life we are going to get at finding true love, so be it wise to carefully not pass them over and waste them, for that may be the one that has been so sought after in the horizons of time.

Old Man

The old man awoke in the morning clutching his wife's robe as it pressed up against his cheek. His body ached and weighed heavy from the unending sorrow. There he lay with his eyes open in a stare remembering her all morning until noon, when he mustered the will to get out of bed.

Dangling his feet over the side of the bed with his head and shoulders slumped over he just sat motionless for a little while. Then he reached over to the dresser and picked up the framed picture of his wife. With his hand he touched her face with his fingertips on the glass as if he was touching her, just as he would sometimes part her hair away from her eyes when he made love to her.

With the frame in hand he tells her, "Your passionate smile always blinded me." He loved her for as long as she lived, and at one time he was the one that waited for her to come back to him. Then he whispers as his lips touch the glass, "I waited for you once before now its you that waits for me on the other side in the horizons of time."

As he places the frame back on the nightstand he inhales deeply, then he holds his breath and sighs, "I discovered the fountain of youth upon loving you, and I will feel and see myself as young as the day I met you, as long as I am thinking of you, even as this body of mine fails me."

The hallway to the kitchen was a short walk, but for him it was a struggle to get there. Walking past the picture frames on the wall, he could see the reflection of himself on the glass next to pictures of her, as he envisioned himself young again. Exhausted as he was, he arrived at the kitchen and sat to rest at the table by a decorative oval shaped mirror with sunflowers carved in the frame. In the mirror he could see the clock on the other wall, as the second hand ticked away counter clockwise. Deformed wax from a long night of burning was all that remained of a red candle at the center of the table. Reminiscing of the candle served to revive him of the dream of being young and writing her that letter long ago in which he expressed to her how much he loved her.

The adventures in his life took him to distant lands with the dreams of being with the woman he loved. It was a journey that passed through desolate places that were surrounded by misery. In that place he found an innocent flower, which he could never bring himself to part with and leave behind. They both needed the woman he loved, because only she could do things for her that only a mother can do with a bond of feminine understand between a woman and a girl, and later one day between a woman and the young woman that she would become. There was a fortune of love that awaited her from a father that dreamed of a family with her and a woman that he loved.

Only the thought of their two children, their two daughters, which they always dreamed of having one day have kept his sprits high. They were both grown women, one with a striking resemblance to their mother, and the other shared her feisty temper. Sundays together on the porch with them and hearing all their dreams and enthusiasm for the future was the happiest day of the week for him. Time passed, and the days and nights grew longer without her by his side, as the weeks turned into months.

One can never predict our future fate, as the old man was ten years older then his beloved wife and he dreaded the thought of one day in the distant future leaving her alone to live without him. The twists and turns of fate had something different in store for them that didn't seem logical and obvious to predict, for it was he that would be the one left behind to live the lonely life of an old man, while he dreamed every day of feeling her love again.

Late one night, after falling asleep in bed with her robe pressed against his cheek and her picture frame by his side, he dreamt he was touching her face and she smiled at him and said, "You don't need the picture frame anymore to caress my face, because time doesn't matter here as there are no more horizons of time."

Author's Comments

At this time I have not completed my course work of clinicals and lectures, so I have not left yet to do volunteer work with Doctors Without Borders, but I will one day. I started writing the book in secret while I was with her, but when our relationship came to an end I continued writing and accordingly made changes to the novel in reflection. You may think the book is all about her, but I actually consider it to be at least just as much about me, because its so much about the person I am, in the way I think and feel, and of my hopes and dreams. The last chapters are a vision of a future that may or may never become reality. Maybe from some desolate place in my heart this is my message in a bottle sent adrift somewhere out there in the horizons of time.

www.ingramcontent.com/pod-product-compliance
Lightning Source LLC
Chambersburg PA
CBHW030346030726
47499CB00003B/929